Rabbids Invasion

Case File #6: Rabbids Road Trip

by David Lewman

illustrated by Shane L. Johnson

Simon Spotlight

New York London Toronto Sydney New Delhi

Based on the TV series Rabbids® Invasion as seen on Nickelodeon™

SIMON SPOTLIGHT
An imprint of Simon & Schuster Children's Publishing Division
1230 Avenue of the Americas, New York, New York 10020
This Simon Spotlight paperback edition September 2015
© 2015 Ubisoft Entertainment. All rights reserved. Rabbids, Ubisoft, and the Ubisoft logo are trademarks of Ubisoft Entertainment in the U.S. and/or other countries. All rights reserved, including the right of reproduction in whole or in part in any form. SIMON SPOTLIGHT and colophon are registered trademarks of Simon & Schuster, Inc. For information about special discounts for bulk purchases, please contact Simon & Schuster Special Sales at 1-866-506-1949 or business@simonandschuster.com.
Designed by Nicholas Sciacca
Manufactured in the United States of America 0815 OFF
10 9 8 7 6 5 4 3 2 1
ISBN 978-1-4814-4114-8 (hc)
ISBN 978-1-4814-4113-1 (pbk)
ISBN 978-1-4814-4115-5 (eBook)

CHAPTER 1:

Leap Rabbid

It all started with a grasshopper.

The grasshopper was doing what grasshoppers do. It was hopping through the grass.

It didn't know it was being watched.

Three Rabbids, those mysterious invaders from who knows where, were watching the grasshopper. When it hopped, they laughed. "BWAH HA HA HA!"

Hopping seemed like a terrific idea! The Rabbids lined up and hopped over each other, following the grasshopper. The grasshopper didn't know it was playing leapfrog with three mysterious invaders from who knows where. It just kept hopping. And so did the Rabbids.

"BWAHP! BWAHP! BWAHP!"

Following the grasshopper, the Rabbids hopped all over the city. They hopped past a bakery. They hopped through a park. They hopped all the way to a small airport on the edge of town.

Out on the runway a plane was getting ready to take off. A young woman stood talking to a man with a clipboard. She wore a green backpack.

The grasshopper hopped right across the runway. It must have gotten tired of hopping and decided to take a short nap, because it hopped up onto the woman's backpack and climbed inside!

From behind a trash can, the Rabbids watched their new friend. Where was he going?

"I'm so excited to be on *The Astonishing Trek!*" the woman said to the man with the clipboard, completely unaware that a grasshopper had just hopped into her backpack. The woman's name was Kelly. "I just know my sister and I are going to win! We're very famous, you know!"

The man nodded, not really listening. He was Bob White, the producer of a TV reality show called *The Astonishing Trek*. On the show, contestants raced across exotic locations all over the world. Bob was checking his list of contestants. Most of them were already at the airport . . . all except for three.

Those three contestants were late. And Bob couldn't wait much longer. The show was on a tight schedule. "Where are those triplets?" he muttered to himself. "We've gotta get going. . . ."

All the contestants this season were unique in some way. The producers had decided to shake things up a bit, and instead of casting regular

people, they cast people who had "a story" to make things even more interesting to the viewers. The producer's clipboard listed this season's special teams of competitors:

Kelly and Karrie, two sisters who were famous for being famous.

Jason Skweeler, a young pop singer, and his assistant, Bill.

Mike Nockowtski, a professional wrestler, and his father/trainer, Mack.

The Visitors, a set of triplets from another country who claimed to be aliens from outer space.

Bob had never seen the triplets, but he'd heard they were really strange looking. He didn't believe for a second that they were aliens. He was just hoping they'd draw in viewers.

Kelly was tired of being ignored by the producer. She decided to go join her sister on the airplane.

The Rabbids watched her go. They knew the grasshopper was still inside her backpack.

One of the Rabbids thought of himself as the group's leader. (Though it wasn't at all clear that the other two Rabbids agreed with him.) He made a decision. Gesturing for the other two Rabbids to follow him, he said "Bwah bwah!" and ran toward the airplane.

The other two Rabbids looked at each other, shrugged, and ran after him.

They didn't know a hidden observer was watching every move they made. . . .

CHAPTER 2:
To Catch a Rabbid

Agent Glyker of the Secret Government Agency for the Investigation of Intruders-Rabbid Division (the SGAII-RD) spied on the Rabbids from behind a bush.

He'd been following the Rabbids since he'd spotted them hopping around the city. He wasn't supposed to be tracking them, though. He was supposed to be at home, because he was on probation from his job at the SGAII-RD. Being on probation wasn't as bad as being fired . . . but it was close.

When his boss returned from his vacation and found out how much damage the Rabbids had caused while Agent Glyker was in charge, he'd immediately called his nephew into his office.

"GLYKER!" he roared. "YOU'RE ON PROBATION!"

"What does that mean?" Agent Glyker had asked his uncle.

DIRECTOR
STERN

"That means you're my sister's kid so I can't fire you right now, but I CAN make you stay at home while we investigate your recent . . ." Director Stern searched for the right word.

"Challenges?" Glyker had suggested.

"DISASTERS! CALAMITIES! CATASTROPHES!" Stern shouted. "NOW GET OUT OF MY OFFICE! DON'T CALL US! WE'LL CALL YOU . . . MAYBE!"

So Agent Glyker had driven his crummy little brown car home to his crummy little apartment and tried to figure out what to do. He'd always wanted to work for the SGAII-RD—there wasn't another job he could think of that he actually wanted. Plus, he didn't want to disobey his uncle's orders. He was in enough trouble already. But then he got an idea. . . .

What if he went rogue?

Instead of just staying at home waiting for Director Stern to let him (maybe) come back to work, he could strike out on his own! When he caught a Rabbid (or two Rabbids! Or three! Three Rabbids would be so great!), his uncle would *have* to let him come back to work! Maybe he'd even get a promotion!

Well, probably not a promotion. His uncle seemed *way* too mad for that.

Still, going rogue seemed worth a try to Agent Glyker.

12

So that's exactly what he did.

Eventually he'd spotted the three Rabbids hopping around the city and followed them all the way out to the small airport.

But NOW what are the Rabbids doing? he said to himself. *Getting on a plane? Why?*

As the three Rabbids ran across the runway toward the plane, the producer thought to himself, *Wow, the Visitors really ARE weird looking!* But Bob didn't say that out loud. He just said, "Hurry, Visitors! You're late! We're about to leave!"

Paying no attention to Bob, the three Rabbids ran right past him, climbed up the stairway, and boarded the plane. "Bwah bwah bwah bwah!"

When he saw the Rabbids get on the plane, Agent Glyker jumped up and ran across the runway, following them. He had to stop them before they flew away! But the producer grabbed his arm before he could follow the Rabbids onto the plane.

"Hold it right there, pal! Who do you think you are?"

"I'm Agent Glyker!" he said before he remembered that he was going rogue. He managed to stop himself before he pulled out his ID and said, "SGAII-RD!"

"Oh, you're the Visitors' *agent*," Bob said. He was impressed. None of the other contestants had agents with them. "Well, they're on board, safe and sound. We'll take it from here."

Glyker thought fast. If he went with the Rabbids on the plane, he could keep track of them. And at the end of the journey, he could capture them!

"As their agent," he said, "I have to go with them."

"Forget it!" Bob said. "Contestants only!"

The pilot leaned out the door of the plane. "The control tower says we've got to leave NOW!"

He said "contestants," Glyker thought to himself. *This must be some kind of contest the Rabbids have wandered into.* Out loud he said, "Either I get on that plane with my clients, or they're out of the contest!"

"Come on, Bob!" the pilot called. "Now!"

Bob White made a quick decision. (That's what good TV producers do.) He didn't want to lose the Visitors as contestants. Now that he'd seen them, he thought they were so strange looking that they were sure to bring more viewers to the show.

"Okay," he said. "Fine. You win. Let's get on that plane!"

As Bob and Agent Glyker ran up the stairs, Bob said, "But no helping your clients! They have to win *The Astonishing Trek* on their own!"

"Understood," Agent Glyker said, smiling. "No help!" To himself he thought, *So the Rabbids are going to compete on* The Astonishing Trek! *I know that show! I used to watch it, until I started working all the time.*

The plane's door slammed shut, and soon it was in the air.

Seconds after the plane left, three odd little men sprinted across the runway. They looked exactly alike, which made sense, as they were triplets. Shading their eyes from the sun, they looked up and saw the plane fly away.

One turned to the other two. "Zweep zop tworp twoop!" All three of them shrugged, and one

pressed a button on a sleek device strapped to his wrist.

Within seconds a spaceship arrived. They climbed onboard and flew back to their home planet, never to return to Earth again.

Where they came from being late didn't matter.

CHAPTER 3:
Rabbids on a Plane

The Rabbids had a wonderful time on the plane.

While Bob and the other contestants read magazines or slept, the Rabbids ran all over the inside of the plane, climbing over seats, crawling under seats, and spending way too much time in the bathroom.

BAM! BAM! BAM! The extreme wrestler, Mike Nockowtski, pounded on the bathroom door. "HEY!" he yelled. "Hurry up! Other people have to go too!"

But he got no answer. All he heard was the sound of splashing water, the toilet flushing, and "BWAH HA HA HA!"

The Rabbids forgot all about the grasshopper they'd been chasing. They were having too much fun climbing into the overhead compartments and going through the other contestants' luggage.

"Dudes!" the pop singer, Jason Skweeler, protested. "That's MY bag! And my clothes!" One of the Rabbids put on a striped shirt. Jason shrugged. "I have to admit, it looks good on you."

A little while later the two sisters, Kelly and Karrie, shivered. "Aren't there any blankets or pillows on this plane?" they whined.

At the back of the plane the Rabbids had made a big pile of all the blankets and pillows. They were leaping off the backs of the seats and landing in the pile. "BWEEEEE!"

Agent Glyker was pretending to sleep but was carefully watching the Rabbids. This was the longest period of time he'd ever spent so close to the invaders, and he wanted to gather all the intel he possibly could. He sneakily took notes:

- The Rabbids are destructive. They've ripped up magazines, napkins, and air-sickness bags.
- They're tougher than they look. When they jump off a seat and miss the pile of blankets and pillows, landing on the floor with a loud thump, they just get up and jump again.
- One of the Rabbids acts like their leader, but the other two Rabbids show their leader very little respect.
- The Rabbids don't show ANYONE respect.
- They love the bathroom.

After many hours the plane finally began to make its descent. Glyker peered out a window, trying to figure out where they were.

Karrie just asked. "Where are we?"

Bob smiled. "You'll find out."

CHAPTER 4:

The Rabbids and the 'Roo

The second the plane landed, the Rabbids pushed past everyone and ran outside. Heat blasted their faces. They looked around. All they saw was sand and scrubby plants.

"Bwoooooh," the leader said.

"Welcome to . . . AUSTRALIA!" Bob said cheerfully.

"Where's the mall?" Kelly asked. "I need nail polish."

Once everyone was out of the plane, Bob told them what the *Astonishing Trek* challenge was going to be. The Rabbids paid no attention, wandering around, picking plants, sniffing them, throwing them at each other, and laughing. "BWAH HA HA HA HA!"

A local man brought Bob a kangaroo. The producer held up a tiny boomerang made out of gold. "See this tiny gold boomerang?" he asked. The boomerang glinted in the bright sunshine. This caught the Rabbids' attention. "Bwooooh," all three of them said. They wanted that shiny thing!

Bob dropped the tiny gold boomerang in the kangaroo's pouch. The man let the kangaroo go, and it hopped away across the wilderness, moving fast with long bounds and leaps.

"First team to bring me the tiny gold boomerang wins this round!"

The Rabbids were off like a shot, sprinting across the hot sand, chasing the kangaroo.

"Hey, no fair!" Karrie said, pointing. "Those weird little Visitors took off before you said 'Go!'"

"Anything goes on *The Astonishing Trek!*" Bob announced. The other three teams took off running after the kangaroo. Glyker started to follow them, but Bob held him back. "Contestants only!" he said sternly. The secret agent would have to wait until the Rabbids came back. He just hoped they *would* come back. . . .

It wasn't easy running through the Australian wilderness. Besides the heat, the ground was uneven, so the contestants had to be careful not to trip over rocks or plants or clumps of dirt or lizards . . .

And the Rabbids weren't making it any easier, either.

When they saw everyone running after them, the Rabbids thought they were being chased. "BWAAAAH!" they yelled, running after the kangaroo even faster. But their legs were short, so very soon Mike, the wrestler, who was in good shape, was catching up with them. Mack, his dad and trainer, urged him on. "Pick up those feet, Mike! Knees high! Go, go, go, go, GO!"

Two of the Rabbids turned around, jumped at Mike, and grabbed onto his legs! "HEY!" he yelled. "GET OFF OF ME!" He didn't want to lose sight of the kangaroo, so he kept running. The two Rabbids loved getting a ride on his legs. "BWAH HA HA HA! BWAH HA!" they laughed.

The other Rabbid wanted a ride too, so he looked around for the nearest leg to jump on. It turned out to be Jason Skweeler's leg. "Dude!" the pop star complained. "Not cool!" He tried shaking the Rabbid off, but it just held on even tighter, laughing. "BWAH HA HA HA!"

Jason turned to his assistant, Bill. "Can't you get this thing off me, Bill?" he asked. Bill shrugged. He was too busy posting tweets for all the pop star's fans to read about how awesome Jason was.

With Rabbids hanging onto their legs, Mike and Jason slowed down, giving Kelly and Karrie a chance to catch up. They cheered each other on. "Go, Kelly!" "Go, Karrie!" "Go, Kelly!" "Go, Karrie!" "YEEEEK!" Karrie had almost stepped on a lizard!

The kangaroo found a small puddle of water to drink from. It stopped by the water and leaned over to get a nice cool drink.

When the Rabbids saw the puddle of water, they jumped off Jason's and Mike's legs and sprinted right into the water. "BWAH HA HA!" They kicked and splashed water on each other. Startled, the kangaroo hopped away.

"You scared him off!" Kelly complained. The Rabbids stared at her, and then started splashing water at her. "Stop it!" she shrieked. They didn't stop. In fact, they started splashing water at *all* the other contestants.

While the other contestants were wiping the water out of their eyes, the Rabbids noticed that the kangaroo had come back to the puddle for a little more water.

The leader Rabbid remembered something, which was very unusual for him. There was something shiny in the kangaroo's pouch!

In a flash the Rabbid ran over to the kangaroo, shoved its hand in the kangaroo's pocket, and pulled out the tiny gold boomerang! The kangaroo hopped away, heading back to the spot where the airplane had landed and its owner was waiting for it.

"BWAH BWAH BWAH BWAAAAAAH!" the Rabbid crowed, holding up the boomerang in triumph!

The other contestants saw the Rabbid holding up the gold boomerang. "Dude," Jason said to Mike. "Are we allowed to take that from him?"

"Bob said anything goes on *The Astonishing Trek!*" Mike growled as he ran toward the Rabbid.

"BWAAAAAH!" the Rabbid screamed when he saw the big wrestler coming at him. He started running back toward the plane. The other two Rabbids ran with him.

When Mike and Jason got close to the Rabbid with the boomerang, the other Rabbids leaped through the air and landed on their legs! "BWEEEEE!" Another fun leg ride!

That slowed Mike and Jason down. Kelly and Karrie weren't even running. They walked back to the plane, looking bedraggled, tired, and angry.

As the Rabbid with the boomerang ran toward the plane, Bob announced, "He's got the boomerang! The Visitors have won this round of *The Astonishing Trek*!"

Glyker couldn't believe it. The Rabbids won? Was winning *The Astonishing Trek* part of their plan to take over the Earth?

The Rabbid with the tiny gold boomerang didn't give it back to Bob. He ran right past the producer, ignoring him, and went up the stairs into the plane. The other two Rabbids jumped off Mike's and Jason's legs and followed him inside.

Mike and his dad and Jason and his assistant just slogged past Bob without saying anything. But when Kelly and Karrie finally arrived, they had plenty to say.

"Those Visitors totally cheated!"

"They jumped on people's legs!"

"They threw water at us!"

"Also, I almost stepped on a LIZARD! SO
GROSS!"

"I found a grasshopper in my backpack!"

As Bob started to repeat that anything goes
on *The Astonishing Trek*, the two angry sisters
interrupted him.

"We'll tell you what's going—US!"

"WE QUIT!"

CHAPTER 5:
Gotta Get a Gondola

Bob spent the whole flight to the next exotic location trying to talk Kelly and Karrie out of quitting. "Just think," he said, "being on this show could make you famous!"

"We're ALREADY famous!" Karrie insisted.

"Yeah, we don't NEED this show!" Kelly said. "Do you know how many fans we have? Like, a zillion!"

It didn't help that while Bob was trying to

convince the two sisters to stay on the show, the Rabbids were throwing the tiny gold boomerang around the inside of the plane. Sometimes it would come back to the Rabbid who threw it. Sometimes it wouldn't. And sometimes it would hit one of the other passengers in the head.

That made the Rabbids laugh the hardest. "BWAH HA HA HA HA!"

The boomerang bonked Kelly in the head. Since it was so tiny, it didn't really hurt, but she was very annoyed. "HEY! CUT IT OUT! THAT IS, LIKE, SO TOTALLY IMMATURE!"

"BWAH HA HA HA HA HA!"

Bob picked up the boomerang and slipped it into his pocket. The Rabbids looked disappointed for a second ("Bwoh . . .") but then got busy raising and lowering all the window shades in the plane.

It was killing Agent Glyker to be so close to the Rabbids but unable to grab them. *What would I do*

39

with them? he thought. *And how would I explain an agent that grabs his own clients? I'll just have to wait until we get back home. The minute we land back at our city's airport, I'll capture all three of the Rabbids! Uncle Jim will have to take me off probation!*

In the meantime Glyker made more notes about the Rabbids:

- The Rabbids love shiny objects.
- They're not afraid of kangaroos.
- They like to splash water.
- They like to ride on people's legs.
- Wherever they come from, there must not be boomerangs.
- They enjoy it when people get bonked on the head.

When the plane landed, they all learned that their next *Astonishing Trek* challenge would be on the canals of Venice!

"Not for us, it won't!" Kelly said as she and her sister stomped off in a huff. "We never want to see those stupid Visitors again!"

They caught the next plane home.

"All right!" Bob said to the three remaining teams, trying to sound positive. "You've got to race across the city to the old clock tower. First team there wins!"

The Rabbids paid no attention to these instructions. They were chasing pigeons in the square, laughing whenever the birds flew. "BWAH HA HA HA!"

"Race how?" Mike the wrestler asked. "Run?"

The producer chuckled. "No, you don't run across Venice. You take the canals. In gondolas!"

Mike, Mack, Jason, and Bill looked around and saw several long, sleek gondolas floating in the canal. Gondoliers stood on the backs of them, waiting for passengers to rent their boats.

The four competitors ran over and jumped into the gondolas, waving their money, rudely cutting in front of a couple on their honeymoon who just wanted a romantic ride. "Hey!" the newlyweds yelled as the *Astonishing Trek* contestants shoved them aside. "No cutting in line!"

Glyker watched the Rabbids to see what they would do. He wouldn't have been at all surprised if they had just gone on chasing the pigeons. Right now that's exactly what they were doing. "BWAH HA HA HA HA!"

But Bob was watching the Rabbids too, concerned

that they weren't taking part in the challenge. He'd already had one team quit on him, and he wasn't about to lose another. Besides, he'd been checking social media, and the Visitors were incredibly popular! Viewers thought they were hilarious!

He got an idea. Bob reached into his pocket and pulled out the tiny gold boomerang. "Oh, Visitors!" he called, holding the boomerang up in the air and waving it so it'd flash in the sunshine. "Remember this?"

The Rabbids looked up from the pigeons on the square. They stared at the boomerang in Bob's hand. "Bwaaaah . . . boohoo."

Bob ran over to a gondola and threw the boomerang in it. "Go get it!" he yelled.

This'll never work,

Glyker thought, watching.

It totally worked.

The Rabbids dashed across the square and jumped into the gondola. Bob tossed a wad of cash to the gondolier standing on the back of the gondola with his long pole reaching into the water. "To the old clock tower!" Bob shouted in Italian. "As fast as you can pole!"

The gondolier looked at the wad of money and grinned. Then he started pushing on his pole as hard as he could, sending the gondola knifing through the water of the canal.

But the other two teams were already far ahead. . . .

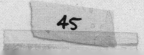

CHAPTER 6:

Sing!

"FASTER!" Mike screamed at the gondolier. "CAN'T YOU GO FASTER?!"

But the gondolier, who spoke only Italian, had no idea what Mike was saying. He kept using his pole to move the gondola through the water slowly and peacefully. He thought maybe Mike wanted him to sing, so he began to croon, *"O, sole mio . . ."*

Mike grabbed his head in frustration.

His dad urged him to breathe. "Deep breaths,

Mikey," he said. "In, out, in, out . . ."

Jason and Bill were several yards behind Mike's gondola. Jason pointed to it, trying to get his gondolier to pass the gondola in front of them. But the gondolier thought Jason meant "You should be singing like that gondolier in front of us." The gondolier was happy to oblige. He was very proud of his beautiful singing voice. "*O SOLE MIO . . .*" he bellowed at the top of his lungs.

Meanwhile, the Rabbids were rapidly gaining on the other two gondolas. They were going faster than any other gondola on the canal! They were about to catch up with the other two *Astonishing Trek* teams. . . .

But the Rabbids didn't notice, because they were still searching the bottom of the boat for the tiny gold boomerang. "BWAH HA!" one of the Rabbids cried, triumphantly holding the boomerang up in the air. He'd found it!

The other two Rabbids looked disappointed that they hadn't been the ones to find the little trinket. They looked at each other and got the same idea at the same time. They turned and jumped on the Rabbid with the boomerang, tackling him! "BWAAAAH!"

"No, no, no, no!" warned the gondolier as the Rabbids wrestled each other for the boomerang. The boat began to tip and sway from side to side, until . . .

SPLOOSH!

The gondolier and all three Rabbids ended up in the canal, with the gondola floating upside down!

The Rabbids didn't seem to mind. They floated on their backs and blew water out of their mouths like fountains. Then they swam over to Jason's gondola and climbed aboard.

"Dudes! No way!" Jason protested. "Get off my gondola! You'll slow us down!"

The Rabbids just ignored the pop singer. But they were fascinated by the gondolier, who was still singing. One of the Rabbids stood in front of the gondolier and struck a pose like his. Then he threw back his head, opened his mouth wide, and started singing loudly. "BWOH BWOH BWAY BWEE BWOH . . ."

Annoyed by this out-of-tune competition, the gondolier sang louder. But the other two Rabbids jumped up and joined their fellow invader. "BWOH BWOH BWAY BWEE BWOH!!!"

Soon tourists strolling along the canal noticed this

odd singing competition. They pointed, laughed,
and recorded the scene with their cameras. Then a
young girl recognized one of the other passengers
in the gondola.

"Hey!" she cried. "THAT'S JASON SKWEELER!"

Other girls along the canal saw she was right.

They couldn't believe it! "Sing for us, Jason!" one of them pleaded. "Please?"

Jason looked at his assistant, Bill. "What should I do?"

"Those are fans, Jason," Bill said. "You should sing!"

So Jason stood up (carefully) and started to sing his most recent hit, "You're So Beautiful I Can Hardly Stand It." The girls along the canal shrieked and screamed!

But the Rabbids took Jason's singing as a challenge. They started singing even louder. "BWOH BWOH BWAY BWEE BWOH!!!!"

The gondolier stopped singing and concentrated on his poling.

Jason tried to outsing the Rabbids. "SO BEAUTIFUL I CAN HARDLY STAND IT . . ." His throat started to ache from singing so loudly.

The three Rabbids ran toward Jason to sing

53

right in his face. But when the front two Rabbids stopped, the third Rabbid didn't know they were stopping, so he kept going . . .

The last Rabbid bumped into the middle Rabbid . . .

The middle Rabbid bumped into the front Rabbid . . .

The front Rabbid bumped into Jason Skweeler and . . .

SPLOOSH!

CHAPTER 7:

A Need for Speed

Jason went right into the canal! "HELP!" he called.
"I CAN SWIM, BUT I DON'T LIKE IT!"

Bill dove into the canal to save
his boss. So did the gondolier
(his company had a strict
policy against letting
passengers drown).

As the two

men swam to the pop singer's rescue, one of the

Rabbids picked up the pole the gondolier had left behind and started pushing it against the bottom of the canal, just the way he'd seen the gondolier do. "BWAH HA!" he cried triumphantly when the boat moved forward through the water.

The other two Rabbids thought pushing the boat along looked fun! They joined their fellow Rabbid, grabbed onto the pole, and helped push. With all three Rabbids pushing the pole, the gondola zipped down the canal! *WHOOSH!*

"BWAH HA HA HA HA!"

Just ahead of them Mike and Mack were still frustrated with the slow pace of their gondola.

Their gondolier continued to be more interested in singing than moving quickly through the water. *"O, sole mio . . ."*

"Is that the only song he knows?" Mike complained.

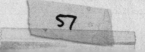

Mack looked behind them.

"Those weird-lookin' little Visitors are gaining on us! Fast!"

"How did they get their gondolier to go faster?" Mike asked.

"They didn't!" Mack replied. "They got rid of him!"

"Good idea!" Mike said. "Why didn't I think of that?"

Using his excellent wrestler's balance, Mike jumped up, moved to the back of the gondola, and picked up the gondolier, who was still singing.

"Sorry about this," Mike said. "But there's a big contest at stake!"

Mike took the gondolier's pole and tossed him into the water. KA-SPLOOSH! Just as the Rabbids were about to pass him, Mike gave the pole a mighty push, shooting his gondola ahead!

"Atta boy, Mike!" his dad cheered. "Remember, use your leg muscles!"

Mike grinned and waved back at the Rabbids. "Bye-bye, Visitors!" he called. "Better luck on your next visit!"

But the Rabbids weren't paying any attention to the ultimate wrestler. They'd noticed something much more interesting in the canal.

A speedboat.

"Bwoooooh . . ."

It was motoring past the Rabbids' gondola. Without even thinking (which seemed to be the way they did just about everything), the three Rabbids leaped from their boat to the speedboat, landing in a tumble of Rabbids.

"Hey!" said the boat owner. "What's the big idea?"

The Rabbids didn't actually *have* an idea, but they were curious. It only took a few seconds for one of them to find the control that made the boat go faster. The Rabbid shoved the handle forward. *VROOM!* The boat zoomed through the water!

At the plaza by the old clock tower Bob and Agent Glyker were waiting for the contestants to arrive. They'd run along the canals, watching the teams race. Bob was peering through binoculars to see who would get there first. Glyker was nervously waiting to see if the Rabbids would show up at all.

To distract himself, he jotted a few more notes:

- The Rabbids can swim!
- The Rabbids like to sing—in their own special way.
- The Rabbids don't hesitate to take over someone else's vehicle.
- The Rabbids seem to enjoy speed.
- They are easily distracted by birds. Or at least pigeons.

"Here they come!" Bob said, pointing.

"All of them?" Glyker asked hopefully, lowering his phone.

"No, just Mike and Mack!" Bob said. "I only see their gondola."

Glyker slumped. He was afraid the Rabbids had disappeared.

"Wait," Bob said. "In that speedboat . . . is that the Visitors?"

Sure enough, a speedboat was zooming through the canal with the three Rabbids on it. Two were being chased around the boat by its owner while the third one pushed the gas throttle forward.

VROOOOM! The speedboat whipped right past Mike's gondola! The waves it made almost capsized the boat.

As they passed the bobbing gondola, the

Rabbids looked toward the plaza in front of the old clock tower, where Bob and Glyker were standing. They saw something very interesting. . . .

As the speedboat came close to the plaza, the three Rabbids jumped out onto the stone walkway! They ran over to . . .

. . . a bunch of pigeons! The pigeons scattered and flew into the air! "BWAH HA HA HA!"

Bob couldn't believe it. "Come on!" he yelled. "There's the old clock tower! It's RIGHT THERE!" He pointed at the historic tower.

But the Rabbids had no interest in the clock tower. They just wanted to chase the pigeons. "BWAH HA HA HA!"

Mike jumped out of his gondola, raced across the plaza to the clock tower, and touched its old wooden door. "We're first!"

"Mike and Mack win this round!" Bob announced.

The Rabbids couldn't have cared less.

65

CHAPTER 8:

Brrrr!

Agent Glyker shivered. It was cold. *Really* cold!

But then, it usually is cold at the North Pole.

Bob was explaining to the remaining contestants that this leg of the competition would require them to race dogsleds to the North Pole.

Only two teams remained: Mike and Mack and the Rabbids. Jason Skweeler had quit in Venice. He was furious that his fans had seen him get dunked in the canal. Not only had they *seen* it, they'd

made videos of him falling into the water and posted them online! Millions of people had seen him calling for help even though he could swim!

So Jason had had enough of *The Astonishing Trek*. Even though Bob had pleaded with him to stay, he'd left the show in Venice.

Bob was pretty worried about only having two teams left. On the other hand, the Rabbids (or the Visitors, as he thought of them) had proved so popular with viewers that the show's ratings were up! Maybe they were really the only team he needed!

"You'll each be given an excellent team of sled dogs and a state-of-the-art dogsled," Bob explained. "First team to the North Pole wins! And since each team has won one leg of the competition already, whoever wins this race wins *The Astonishing Trek*!"

"All right!" Mike said, pumping his fist.

The Rabbids paid no attention to Bob's little speech. They were busy playing with the sled dogs—crawling under their bellies and trying to climb onto their backs. When the dogs barked, the Rabbids barked back. "BWARF! B W A R F ! BWARF!"

Agent Glyker walked up to Bob. "So after this race we can go home?"

"Yes," Bob said, nodding.

"But until you get your clients onto that dogsled, they're not going anywhere! We'll stay here as long as it takes until we get a good race!"

Mike and Mack had already climbed onto their sled and taken off. "Mush!" Mike yelled, since he'd seen a movie once where that was what you said to sled dogs. He didn't know why "mush" made the dogs run, but it seemed to work. The dogs took off, speeding down the snowy path toward the North Pole.

The Rabbids, meanwhile, were still playing with their team of dogs. They were delighted to find that they could make the dogs howl just by howling themselves. "BWOOOH!" "AROOOH!" "BWOOOH!" "AROOOH!"

Agent Glyker knew he had to get the Rabbids onto that sled. Otherwise, who knew when they'd get back home? And if he didn't get home and take the Rabbids into the SGAII-RD soon, Director Stern might forget all about him and just leave him on probation permanently!

Glyker squared his shoulders, full of determination. Those crazy Rabbids *were* getting on that dogsled!

Glyker knew something about Rabbids. When you chased them, they ran away. Usually. Unless they didn't. But it was worth a try.

Lifting his arms over his head, Agent Glyker ran at the Rabbids, roaring! "ROOOAAAARRR!"

The Rabbids looked up, startled. One of them looked like he was going to laugh, but the leader jumped onto the sled. "Bwah bwah!" he called to the other two. They climbed onto the sled too.

That was just what Glyker and Bob wanted to see. "MUSH!" they both yelled.

The dogs took off down the icy path with the Rabbids holding on for dear life. Once they really got going, the Rabbids enjoyed the wild ride. "BWEEEE!"

Because the three Rabbids were smaller and lighter than the big wrestler and his dad (who was also a big guy), they soon caught up with the other dogsled.

"MUSH!" yelled Mike and Mack.

"BWAAAA!" yelled the Rabbids.

The two dogsleds sped on, side by side, zipping over the snow and ice. With their weight advantage, the Rabbids were slowly pulling ahead.

"There it is!" Mack shouted, pointing ahead. "The North Pole!"

But something big and white stood between the two teams and their goal. And it wasn't a pile of snow.

It was a polar bear!

When the dogs saw the bear, they screeched to a halt! The Rabbids went flying off their sled, and so did the wrestler and his dad! They all tumbled into the snow, landing near where the polar bear stood.

The dogs turned around and ran back the way they'd come.

The polar bear stood on its back legs and roared! "GROAARR!"

"Nice bear . . ." Mike said, holding his hands up in a calming gesture.

The Rabbids just stood there, staring. They'd never seen a polar bear before!

The huge white bear looked at the two humans. Then it looked at the three Rabbids. And to the bear, the small white creatures looked a lot like . . . polar bear cubs!

So the bear charged right at the humans!

"YAAAAAAAH!" screamed Mike and Mack as they turned and ran away. The bear chased them for a little while, then turned aside and headed home. But they didn't know that. They ran all the way back to the base camp.

Would the Rabbids go on and make it to the North Pole, winning this race and *The Astonishing Trek*?

After the dogs, the humans, and the polar bear left, the three Rabbids stood in the snow looking around. The Northern Lights flashed across the sky.

The Rabbids saw the North Pole, but it didn't really interest them. It was just a pole.

But then they looked a little closer . . .

Bob the producer had worried that the Visitors might not stay interested in the pole he'd installed at the finish. They seemed to have very short attention spans. So he'd done something very clever. . . .

80

When the Rabbids looked at the pole more closely, they saw that it had *three* tiny gold boomerangs attached to it!

"BWAH HA!" they cried, running toward the pole.

And as the three of them touched the pole, each grabbing a boomerang for himself, Bob and Agent Glyker rode up on a snowmobile.

"Looks like we have a winning team!" Bob cried, delighted.

CHAPTER 9:
Winners and Losers

"The Secret Government what?" Bob asked, looking at the badge Glyker was holding up.

"The Secret Government Agency for the Investigation of Intruders, Rabbid Division."

They were standing on the runway of the airport back home. The Rabbids were still inside the plane, flushing the toilet. Bob and Glyker could hear them laughing. "BWAH HA HA HA!"

"What are Rabbids?"

"*They* are," Glyker said, gesturing toward the plane. "The Visitors. They're invading our planet. So I'm taking them into custody. Right now."

Bob frowned. "Now wait a minute! Those Rabbids just happen to be the new stars of my show! You're not taking them anywhere!"

"Oh, yes I am!" Glyker insisted.

As the two men argued, they failed to notice a strange-looking spaceship silently land behind them. It looked like a flying submarine with a face on the front. A Rabbid face . . .

"Maybe I should arrest you, too!" Glyker yelled.

"On what charge?" Bob shouted back.

"Interfering with an official government investigation!" Glyker said, even though he was pretty sure he didn't have the authority to do that. Especially while he was on probation.

"You wouldn't dare!" Bob countered. "I'd have my lawyers on you so fast . . ."

Behind them the three Rabbids cheerfully slipped out of the plane and into the spaceship.

Glyker and Bob whipped around. "Wait!" they cried. "No!"

But the spaceship flew into the sky and disappeared.

Agent Glyker sighed. Uncle Jim wasn't going to like this one bit. He turned to Bob.

"So," he said, "are you looking for new *Astonishing Trek* contestants?"

Bob raised an eyebrow.

And a grasshopper hopped by.

87

Glyker's To-Do List:

1. Buy a warm jacket in case I ever have to return to the North Pole.

2. Take swimming lessons—Rabbids are good swimmers!

3. Ask mom to bake another cake for Uncle Jim—maybe use sprinkles this time.

4. Research alternate career options just in case Uncle Jim refuses to end probation period (or if the cake doesn't help).

5. Post picture with Jason Skweeler to social media. #CoolGlyker

large mouth